Ten in the Den

For Joshua James
J. B.

Ω

Published by
PEACHTREE PUBLISHING COMPANY INC.
1700 Chattahoochee Avenue
Atlanta, Georgia 30318-2112
www.peachtree-online.com

Text and illustrations © 2005 by John Butler

First published in Great Britain in 2005 by Orchard Books
First United States edition published in 2005
First United States trade paperback edition published in 2016

Printed in May 2019 in China
10 9 8 7 6 5 4 3 2 (hardcover)
10 9 8 7 6 5 4 3 2 (trade paperback)

HC ISBN: 978-1-56145-344-3
PB ISBN: 978-1-56145-965-0

www.johnbutlerart.com

Library of Congress Cataloging-in-Publication Data

Butler, John, 1952-
Ten in the den / written and illustrated by John Butler.— 1st ed.
p. cm.
Summary: One by one nine forest creatures fall out of bed when Little Mouse says "Roll over!"
ISBN 1-56145-344-7
1. Nursery rhymes. 2. Children's poetry. [1. Animals—Poetry. 2. Counting. 3. Nursery rhymes.] I. Title.
PZ8.3.B9788 Te2005
[E]—dc22
2004026868

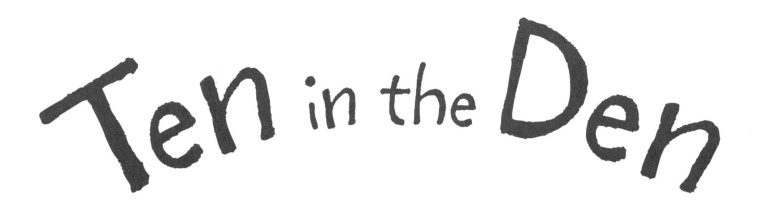

Ten in the Den

John Butler

PEACHTREE
ATLANTA

There were **ten** in the den,
and the little mouse said,

"Roll over! Roll over!"
So they all rolled over and . . .

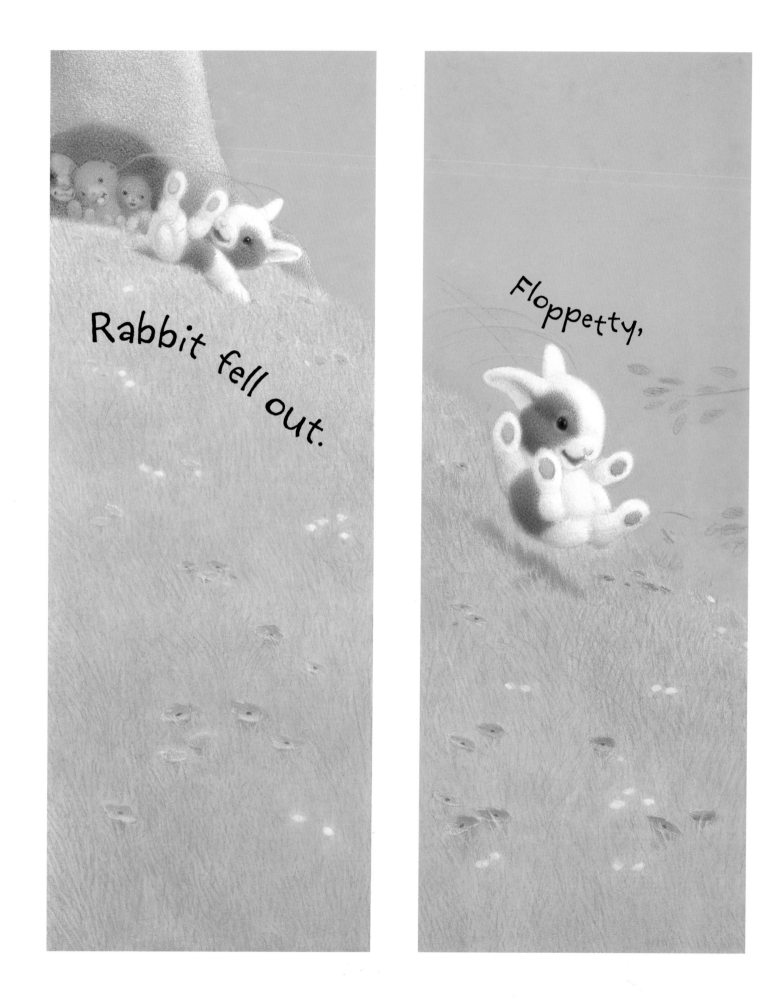

hoppetty,

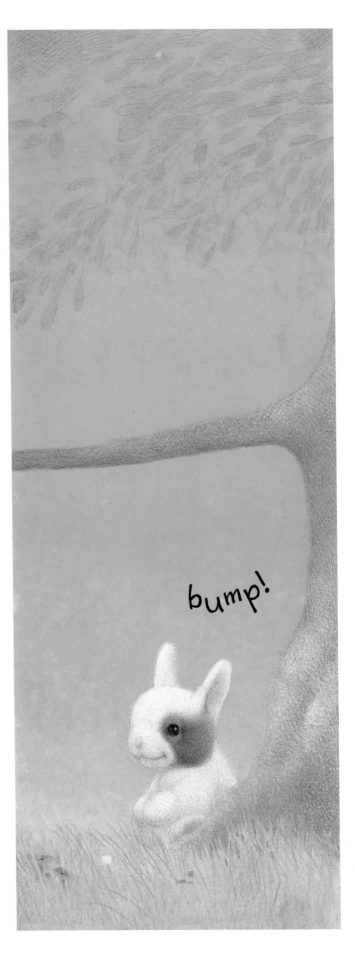

bump!

There were **nine** in the den,
and the little mouse said,

"Roll over! Roll over!"
So they all rolled over and . . .

Mole fell out.

Roly,

Poly,

bump!

There were **eight** in the den,
and the little mouse said,

"Roll over! Roll over!"
So they all rolled over
and Beaver fell out.

slippy,   slidey,
        bump!

There were **seven** in the den,
and the little mouse said,

"Roll over!
Roll over!"

So they all rolled over and . . .

Badger fell out.

Bouncy,

pouncy,

bump!

There were **six** in the den,
and the little mouse said,

"Roll over! Roll over!"
So they all rolled over and . . .

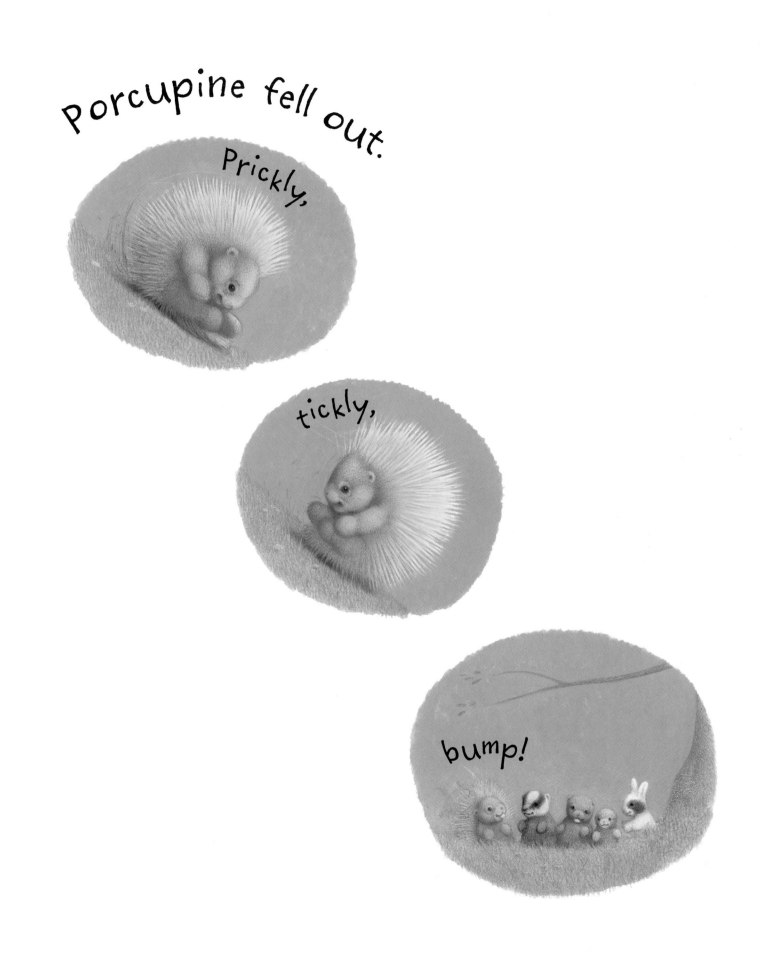

Porcupine fell out.
Prickly,
tickly,
bump!

There were **five** in the den,
and the little mouse said,

"Roll over! Roll over!"
So they all rolled over and . . .

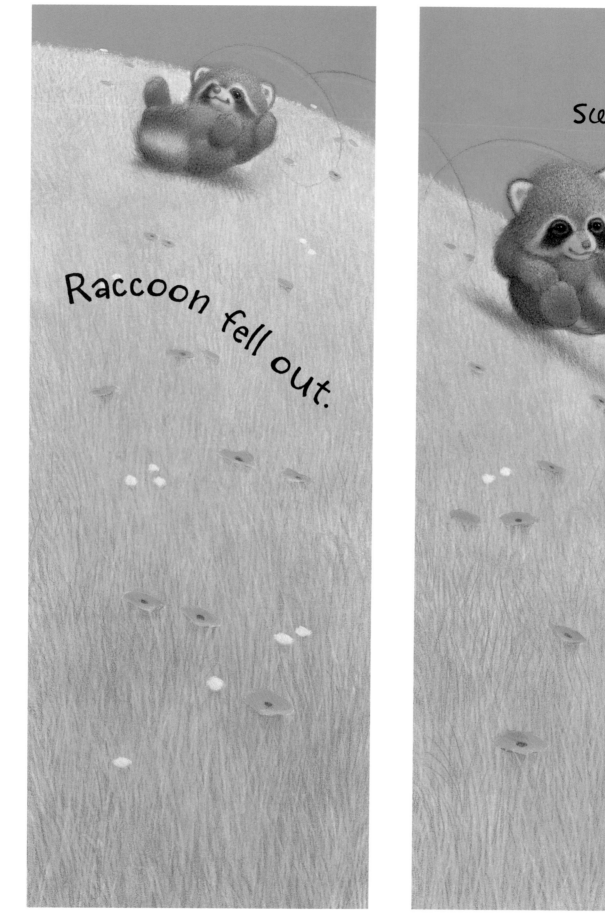

Raccoon fell out.

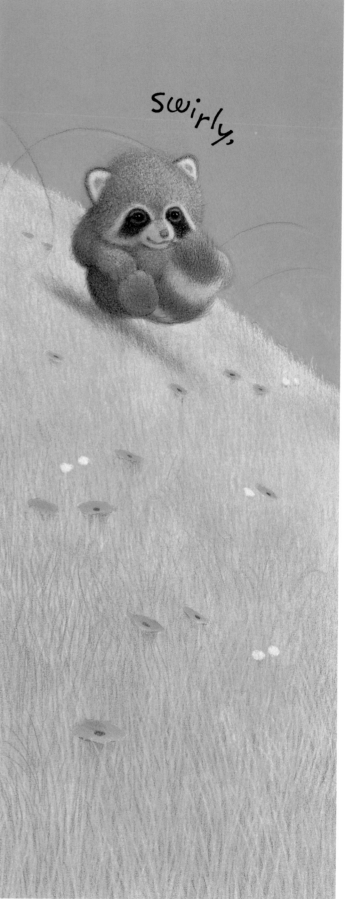

Swirly,

There were **four** in the den,
and the little mouse said,

"Roll over! Roll over!"
So they all rolled over and . . .

Fox fell out.

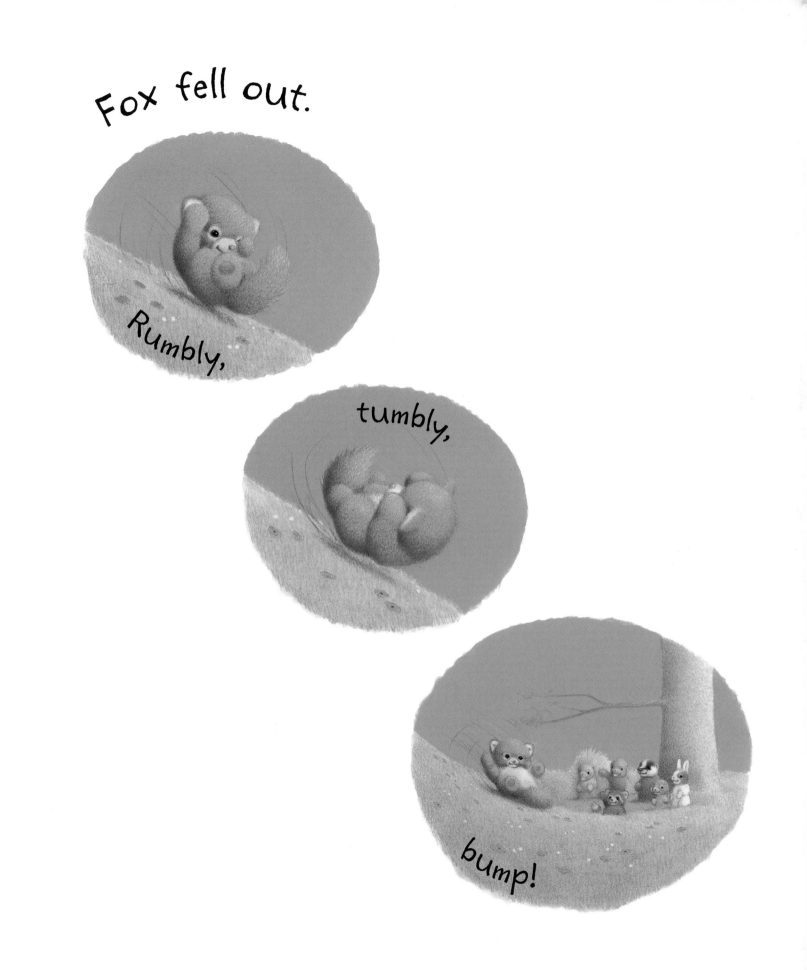

Rumbly,

tumbly,

bump!

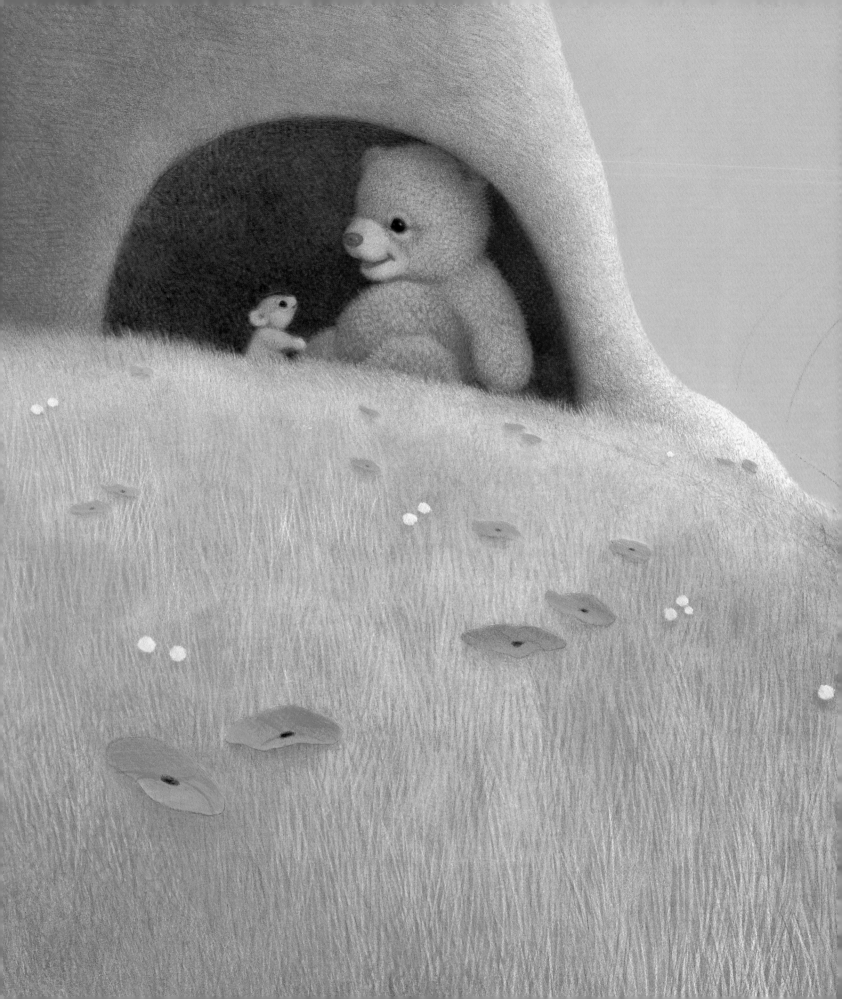

There were **three** in the den,
and the little mouse said,

"Roll over! Roll over!"

So they all rolled over
and Squirrel fell out.

squiggly,

wiggly,

bump!

Bear fell out.

Bumpety, thumpety,

There were **two** in the den,
and the little mouse said,

"Roll over!
Roll over!"

So they both rolled over and . . .

bump!

There was **one** in the den,
and the little mouse sniffed,

"I miss my friends!"

So he rolled over and scampered out.

"Wait

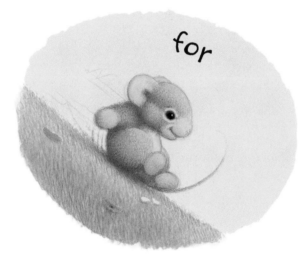

for

me!"

There were **ten** friends again,
and the little mouse yawned . . .

"Night night.
Sleep tight!"

So they all snuggled together and . . .

fell fast asleep.
ZZZzzzzzzzzzzzzzzz